ORPHAN OLLIE OPTS IN

Mario E. Lombardo

This book is a work of fiction. Any resemblance to actual events or persons, living or dead, is entirely coincidental.

"Orphan Ollie Opts In," by Mario E. Lombardo. ISBN 978-1-63868-116-8 (softcover).

Published 2023 by Virtualbookworm.com Publishing Inc., P.O. Box 9949, College Station, TX 77842, US. ©2023, Mario E. Lombardo.

FAMOUS ORPHANS

ACTORS:
CHARLIE CHAPLIN, MARLENE DIETRICH, MARILYN MONROE

ARTISTS:
EDGAR DEGAS, RAPHAEL

AUTHORS:
EDWARD ALBEE, DANTE, EDGAR ALLAN POE, GERTRUDE STEIN, LEO TOLSTOY

ENTREPRENEURS:
ARTHUR ANDERSEN, L.L. BEAN, COCO CHANEL, STEVE JOBS

FIRST LADY:
ELEANOR ROOSEVELT

PRESIDENTS:
HERBERT HOOVER, ANDREW JACKSON, JAMES MONROE

SCIENTIST:
GEORGE WASHINGTON CARVER

SPORTSMEN:
BABE RUTH, JIM THORPE

STATESMEN:
FREDERICK DOUGLASS, ALEXANDER HAMILTON, JOHN HANCOCK

VOCALISTS:
RAY CHARLES, ELLA FITZGERALD, EARTHA KITT

RESPECTFUL APPRECIATION

Many thanks to Gilbert D. Bloom, A. Jack Gabig, Robert M. Gullo, and Ralph S. Martini, each of whom reviewed a draft and provided valued insights and suggestions.

DEDICATION

To the more than 100,000 children in United
States waiting for adoption.

1.

I collapsed in a kitchen chair, mentally and physically exhausted, and took a long deep breath. It was finally over, the neighbors all gone. They tidied up the place before leaving and my best friend's mom told me that she and Christopher, her husband, would stop over in the morning to talk a little about the future.

The future, what future, I thought. I'm sixteen and all alone now. Never seen my Dad; only know he died in Nam. And now no Mom. A Mom who lived a hardscrabble life sacrificing for me. And for years crying at night behind the closed bedroom door. I heard her. And vowed I would get a good-paying job when I grew up so she finally could get some rest.

Single momhood is the pits. Yea, I know I'm not the only kid who lived with a single mom. And that the world is filled with single moms. But, I don't give a hoot about them. I only care about my Mom. But, tell me. Why did God let her die? Explain that to me. What good did that do? Damn it, God. We were doing fine. I was enjoying 10th grade and Mom liked her cashier job at the neighborhood grocery store. What am I going to do without my Mom? I have nobody now. My face is wet with tears as I sob uncontrollably.

The next morning Luke's parents, Mr. and Mrs. Armenti, came over as promised and discussed what would happen next. They had contacted the local Child Services Agency and were told that I would receive a visit this very afternoon from someone from that office who would interview me and answer any questions I had.

That afternoon, as expected, Ms. Catelin, a social worker from the Savannah Agency, stopped by and asked a bunch of questions. My age, height, weight, school grade, and interests, all of which she dutifully wrote down in a notebook. She then told me Mr. Goldman would visit tomorrow morning to lay out all available options for placement, answer questions, and record my preferences. She took a couple of photos, wished me good luck, and then left.

My head was spinning, things were all happening too fast. I was confused and scared and thought I had better start thinking about what to do. I'm not sure I wanted some strangers mapping out my life.

Luke stopped by later and said he overheard his parents talking about adopting me. He said he loved the idea that we could become brothers. Wow, I told him, I am really getting confused about the lightning speed of what's happening. I told him that I needed to think things over a bit. Luke understood and asked me to not do anything rash, and to hear what the State Agency folks had to say before deciding anything. He then suggested I should also talk with Father Gullo at Mercy Church to get his advice.

I tossed and turned in bed that night, awakening when I heard a loud knocking on the door. I jumped up, slipped on a pair of jeans, and let Mr. Goldman in. He was a pleasant man, who informed me about available options, including adoption, a foster home, or an all-boys orphanage. I had seen movies about life in foster homes and orphanages and was not sure that I wanted any part of those places. Then I remembered Luke's suggestion to seek the advice of our parish priest, Father Gullo.

2.

"How are you holding up, Ollie?" asked Father Gullo.

"Ah, I'm a little better now Father, thanks, but need some advice on what I should do next."

"Well, Ollie, you have choices. In addition to Georgia's various Group Homes Program, I am very familiar with Boys Town in St. Augustine, Florida, as well as the Milton Hershey School in Hershey, Pennsylvania. Boys Town is Catholic and is headed by Father Augustine and Milton Hershey is nonsectarian so you will be free to attend Catholic services and it is headed by Mr. Gabig. Both places have wonderful educational resources with two discrete tracks: academic or vocational. I have had experience with both places and each will prepare you to become a productive member of society when you leave. Ollie, the reality is only a very small percentage of adoptions occur at your age so you will need to acquire a skill to get a job when you leave."

"Well, Father, is one place better than the other?"

"Both are more than a century old with sterling national reputations."

"But, what about the entrance fee Father, I only have a $2,000 life insurance check?"

"Ollie, Mercy has an emergency fund established to assist its parishioners in times of need so don't worry about that. However, Ollie, you will be expected to participate in the Town's offsite work program to earn your stay once there."

"Okay, Father, sounds great, the sooner I get on with my life the better. And since both are comparable, I'll opt for Boys Town and the warmer climate of Florida."

"Are you sure? Don't you want to think about it for a while."

"No, Father, Boys Town sounds like the right choice for me."

"Settled then, I'll call Father Augustine and get back to you Ollie."

"Thanks for your help, Father."

Father Gullo called me the next day and told me Boys Town could and would accommodate me. I thanked the good Father, then went to see Luke, told him and his parents of my plans, and thanked them for their help and kindness. Went home, packed some clothes, and took the next Greyhound bus to St. Augustine and my new home. My Mom and I vacationed there one summer and we loved everything it had to offer.

3.

"Welcome to Boys Town, Ollie, I am Father Augustine, Father Gullo phoned to give me the good news that you were coming."

Father Augustine was in his late 40s, tall and lean, nice looking with a snowy white shock of hair, dark blue eyes, and an athletic well-toned tanned physique. My guess was he was a firm, no-nonsense man. His handshake was firm and his eyes were fixated on mine reminding me of that bald eagle at the Savannah Zoo who scared the bejeebers out of me when I was little.

"Your room is 314 Ollie and dinner is at 6. We can talk tomorrow morning at 9 and I'll fill you in on everything then."

I thanked him for his welcome and headed out the door and up the stairs looking for room 314. There was no elevator in the building.

Room 314's door was open so I walked in and saw one bed with some stuff on it and the other neatly made, undisturbed, and assumed it was mine. As I was unpacking and settling in, my roommate walked in and introduced himself. He was about 5 feet tall, slender, and clearly a featherweight. He had coal black hair, and dark brown eyes with unusually long eye lashes that curled upward like the artificial lashes women buy for their eyelids. With a broad warm smile, he extended his hand to greet me. My first impression: I think I was going to like him.

"Hi, I'm Victor, your roommate. Welcome to the Town. It will be nice having a roommate for my final year here. I hope we can become close friends."

"Hi, I'm Ollie, nice meeting you Victor."

We then sat on our beds and I asked Victor about Father Augustine. He said he was a nice man, firm but fair, and the door to his office was always open. "And rumor has it, he was an All-State football player in high school. That's about it. Don't know much more about him."

Victor then asked where I was from and if I had any brothers or sisters. I told him I was from Savannah, Georgia and I was the only one left in my family, that both of my parents were dead.

He volunteered that he had no siblings either, that his mom was also deceased, but that his Dad was living in Pittsburgh. When I asked him why he was here if he was not an orphan, he shrugged his shoulders and said that was a story for another day. He then quickly added it was dinner time and he was famished.

Hmm, I wondered what that was all about.

I followed Victor down the hall to the floor's only bathroom to wash our hands before going down to the dining hall on the main floor. I was starving and ate a huge bowl of spaghetti with the maximum allotted two meat balls. Make that three meat balls, one was donated by Victor who didn't seem to eat that much, even though he was "famished." But, I welcomed the extra meatball. And my first impression was right. I knew Victor and I would get along just fine.

4.

Promptly at nine the next morning, I met with Father Augustine. He first gave me a brief historical overview of Boys Town, saying it was founded in the early 1900s by a Catholic priest named Flanagan and today it has nine sites in the United States.

He made it clear that the Town's goal is to give each boy an opportunity to develop into a responsible young man who will contribute to society when he graduates at age 18. He then gave me a feel for what is expected of me: check the bulletin board every morning to see the day's assignments beginning at 7 A.M. (including cleanup duties at the kitchen, hallways, latrines, and the common grounds); keep myself and my room neat and clean; attend breakfast at 8, mass at 9, and classes from 9 to 12; leave the campus after lunch to work in one of the local businesses that partner with Town; and contribute 90% of my earnings to Town as payment for my room and board.

After dinner, it was recreational time, free to do whatever I wished, with lights out at ten. He asked me if I had any questions and I told him only one at this time, which was did I need to make an appointment to see him in the future. He smiled and said "No appointments necessary. Just drop by and look into the open door to see if I am free." I left the office liking Father Augustine.

I headed for the bulletin board to check job openings, saw one offering a cashier position in a pizza shop so I tore off one of the finger-like-tear-aways at the bottom of the ad. It listed the owner's name, address, and telephone number. I decided to check it out.

5.

The "Mom and Pop Pizza Shop" was a small pizza carryout place on a cobbled street near Flagler College. It occupied the first-floor front of a small brick bungalow. Mr. Martini, the owner, looked over the one-page application he asked me to fill out and asked if I was available until 10 P.M., 6 days a week. The shop was closed on Sunday. Although I would miss the dinner hour at Home, I reasoned I loved pizza and wouldn't mind eating it every night. I told him I was available. Mr. M then offered me the job on a trial basis. "What do you say, Ollie?"

"Yes, I'll take it, thank you so much Mr. M, and I promise you will not be sorry."

Back in my room, I told Victor the good news. He was happy for me and cautioned that I should let Father Augustine know about the skipping of dinners.

"Oh, God I hope I didn't goof, I accepted the job."

"Nah, not a problem, a lot of the guys work late and miss dinner. It's just that Father Augustine likes to know our whereabouts. By the way Ollie, the bulletin board schedule has you on latrine duty this Friday."

"Yipes, on my first week of working."

"Don't worry about it, I'll take your place. I'm off this Friday from the hospital." I thanked Victor and told him I owed him one and he nodded his head in agreement.

6.

My first week at the shop flew by. I enjoyed working with Mr. M. He was patient, fair, and complimentary of my hustle and "especially my mannerly way with the customers." We were developing into an efficient team. I was responsible for taking the orders, handing the boxed pizzas to customers, and operating the cash register. Mr. M made the pizzas and boxed them. He was a whiz at both. I learned that Mrs. Martini had died of cancer recently and I was, in effect, taking her place in the shop. I also learned that Mr. M had let two previous hirees go after their trial periods. I was determined that was not going to happen to me.

7.

The morning "white collar" and "blue collar" courses in Town were taught by volunteer college professors and construction and maintenance instructors. The classes were stimulating and triggered a high degree of group discussion. There were only three required core courses, Basic English, Basic Math, and Elementary Theology, the latter taught by Father Augustine. The rest of the courses were elective. This format was designed to allow us the freedom of choosing an academic or vocational career path upon graduation. Father Augustine had designed the curricular program and was pleased with its success. The reputation of Town graduates among the partnering local businesses was excellent.

Victor was already excelling in the academic path. He was determined to attend college after graduation and then med school. I knew I was a klutz when it came to anything mechanical so the vocational path was not an option for me. I simply defaulted to the academic track not knowing yet what I was going to be doing for a living.

8.

After two or three weeks, I became comfortable with my daily Town routine: Bulletin Board, Mass, Chore, Breakfast, School, Lunch, Chore, Work, Dinner (Sundays), Shower, Rest, Rec, Free, Chapel, Sleep.

Our chapel was not like the beautiful Cathedral Basilica in the Historic District. No, not close. It was not even a stand-alone building. Our chapel was a converted long and narrow windowless room on the first floor of our Home next to the kitchen. A plain wooden crucifix hung behind the altar, rows of wooden benches as pews, and an interior so dark and quiet the word throughout the Town was Jesus could hear our prayers even if we were mumbling. But, as Father Augustine often remarked, the chapel was functional and fulfilled its purpose.

I spent a good bit of my free time in the chapel talking to Mom about how much I missed her. I also admitted I was angry with God for taking her away from me. But I told her as time passed, I was sorry and ashamed of my emotional blasphemes and confessed everything to Father Augustine. Then, I quickly changed the subject and told her how happy I was in my new Home. I told her about my new job and how I liked the owner, Mr. M; about Victor, my friend and roommate; and about Father Augustine's caring presence and leadership---a perfect role model for us kids.

9.

I fell into a comfortable rhythm working with Mr. M. Business was thriving. Pizza sales were spurting upwards month after month. Mr. M often kidded me about the sudden spike in young teeny-bopper traffic, especially Rosie Fernandez, the cute high-schooler who seemed to stop by the shop quite often after school. When I asked Mr. M how he knew her name, he said that St Augustine was a small town and everyone pretty much knew everyone, that he knew the Fernandez family from the Basilica.

Rosie was a senior at St Augustine High and I knew she had a crush on me even though we had not really said much to each other. She would say "Hi", order a slice of plain cheese pizza, and take it outside and sit on the bench across the cobbled street from the shop. She sat there on purpose knowing I could see her from the huge shop window.

On a recent pleasant afternoon, an auspicious event happened. Not being busy, I mentioned to Mr. M that I was going to step outside a minute or two to chat with Rosie. I had remarked to Mr. M that I probably was the only 16 year old in St Augustine who had never dated and the time had arrived.

Mr. M just smiled and flicked his hands with a "go" "go" scoot wave.

During the past year, Rosie and I often had exchanged pleasantries in the shop but nothing more. But I knew I liked what I saw: she was petite, had thick dark black hair framing her cute face, which lit up with lovely dark eyes and a warm "made you melt" smile. Wasting no time, I asked her if she would like to see a movie at the Corazon Theater on Sunday. She said she would love to and volunteered that she had never been on a real date. "That makes two of us." We both smiled and relaxed upon sharing that news and chatted nonstop as if we knew each other since birth. Rosie gave me her phone number and address before departing. A customer was arriving so I needed to return to work.

10.

On Saturday, I told Victor about my date and he quickly asked if Rosie had a girlfriend whom he could date. I told him that I didn't really know but that I would ask her on Sunday.

I was anxious to see her again and felt Sunday would never arrive.

Sunday: I took the Cordova Street bus to Rosie's home and rang the doorbell. Rosie answered the door looking lovely. A tiny shockwave rippled through my body when I saw her. "You look pretty," I blurted. She thanked me and then introduced me to her mom, dad, and younger sister and brother. As we started to leave, Mr. Fernandez reminded her of her 10:30 curfew saying it, I felt, more for my benefit than Rosie's.

We walked to the nearby Cordova Street bus stop, hopped on the bus, and conversed all the way to the cinema stop. After the movie, we stopped at a nearby ice cream shop and indulged in huge hot fudge sundaes. We were laughing as we chatted over the sundaes clearly enjoying each other's company. I told her about Victor suggesting a double date in the future with one of her girlfriends. She asked me to tell her a little about him, which I did, after which she said her good friend Margrete would be a perfect match for Victor.

Walking to the bus stop to return home, I extended my hand downward near Rosie and she grasped it and gave it a little squeeze. We looked at each other and smiled but said nothing and kept walking hand in hand. The bus ride home was pure happiness and excitement knowing I had found someone special.

When we reached the door of her home, we faced each other, looked into each other's eyes, but I was unsure whether I should kiss her goodnight. I didn't want to rush things and spoil the evening. So, I asked her "Will it be okay if I kiss you?" Rosie looked at me, nodded her approval, and said "Yes, please do."

When I arrived back at the House, Victor was waiting for me in the Rec room. "Well, did you have a good time?"

"Yes."

"Good, did Rosie have a friend for me?"

"Yes."

"Ah, come on" he said to me "quit kidding around and fill me in."

I told Victor all I know is her name is Margrete.

"Oh, that's a pretty name, when do we double date?"

I told Victor that I was beat and was going up to bed. He said he was tired also and walked up the stairs with me peppering me with follow up questions, such as, did I kiss Rosie or not?

"Yes, Victor, now let's hit the sack."

Once in bed, I slowly savored and rehashed everything Rosie and I did on the date. Especially the kiss at the end.

11.

Rosie and I began to see each other often and we soon became a couple. On Sundays, we spent our afternoons at St Augustine or Crescent Beach and our evenings catching a movie or a play at Flagler. On occasion, Victor and Margrete joined us. He told me he liked everything about Margrete. And, I could see that Margrete immediately took a liking to him also. Rosie and I agreed they soon would become a couple.

After months of steady dating, our relationship progressed from the "Like" stage to the more serious "Loke" stage. We shared more personal information about each other. I told her of my Mom's sudden death, my period of grief and fear, my decision not to go to a State-sponsored home, and my reason for selecting St Augustine and Boys Town.

Rosie in turn filled me in or her early school years and how, at times, some kids would call her ugly names and tease her about her Mexican heritage and the fact that her family lived in a city-subsidized apartment building. Her Mom and Dad had emigrated from Mexico when she was a year old. She said she was looking forward to her 18th birthday when she could initiate the naturalization process to become a citizen. Both of her parents had become naturalized citizens and were working. She volunteered her father was employed by the City Park Service and her mother as a short-order chef at Flagler College.

We comforted each other as we talked.

12.

It was December. Christmas was around the corner and our Home was electric with excitement. We were looking forward to the Home's annual Christmas party. I learned from Father Augustine that for some of the boys, it would be their first experience with Christmas traditions. The Rec Room was decorated with a huge ceiling-high fir tree loaded with colorful home-made ornaments and twinkling white lights. Under the tree on Christmas day, each of us of the Town "family" would find a token gift from Santa a/k/a Father Augustine.

I asked Victor if he was going home to Pittsburgh to celebrate the holiday with his Dad. He said "No" and when I asked him why not he started to tear.

"Whoa there, Victor, what's this all about."

"Ollie, the truth is my Dad is ashamed of me, wanted me out of his life, and sent me here so he wouldn't have me around anymore. I couldn't do anything to please him. I was on the school honor roll and also president of student council but he just didn't like me. You see, Ollie, he was an All-Pro football player. Played linebacker for the Steelers and lived in, and for, the world of sports. And when he saw that I couldn't even catch a ball, any type of ball, or wasn't interested in athletics at all, he said mean and ugly things like he always wondered if I were really his son, or, he could not believe I had his genes. Or, I was so damn girlish with my long eyelashes that I should go play jacks with the girls in the neighborhood, and I should stay out of his sight until he could find a place to put me."

Victor was sobbing, "Ollie, when you know your Dad is disgusted with you, and can't stand even looking at you, you are in a very dark and lonely place. And ashamed. I haven't told anyone, not even Father Augustine. I honestly feel like a real orphan. No, Ollie, I definitely will not be invited home for Christmas."

I was a little stunned, didn't know quite what to say, so I just hugged his shaking body and then left him alone crying in our room.

I don't know which is worse: never having a Dad in your life to love you or having a Dad in your life who doesn't love you.

13.

The pizza sales were on the upswing and Mr. M said he was pleased with my work ethic. Our business relationship had spilled over to a personal one over time, with Mr. M occasionally inviting first me, then later, me and Victor over for dinners. My work status was looking promising and I needed to talk with Rosie about our future together.

Our relationship had grown stronger through the "Loke" stage and we were now solidly in the "Love" stage. So, on her 18th birthday, I surprised her with a silver signet ring with a "21" inscribed on the ring's distinguishable flat top. "Creating a lifetime commitment" I uttered, as I placed the ring on her finger. She acknowledged our engagement by giving me a long tight hug and a kiss on the cheek. We were pleased with each other and only time stood in the way of marriage.

To celebrate our engagement, Frank and Mary Fernandez held a family dinner party at their apartment. They also invited Mr. M who readily accepted. It was an enjoyable evening and made Rosie feel especially good that her parents liked me.

But the bombshell surprise of the night occurred when Mr. M stunned everyone by announcing that if I remained at the shop after graduation, then he would offer me a 10% ownership interest in the business and a temporary rent-free residence in his house until I could afford a place of my own. I looked at Mr. M and he was smiling broadly and extended his right hand for me to shake. I ignored the hand and flung myself into his arms and hugged him in appreciation. What a decent caring man. I never knew my father but Mr. M was a wonderful substitute.

The next week was filled with exciting news. I was accepted into Flagler's business school and would be attending at night. And Rosie was excited about becoming a U.S. citizen erasing the little black cloud that hovered over her for 18 years of her life.

Years flew by. I was busy working in the shop during the day and attending school at night. I was on a tight budget so I could start saving for a home of our own. Our social life consisted of doing mostly free stuff such as going to the beaches, or visiting the local museums and historic sites. Just being with each other was exciting enough. Some nights we just sat under the palm trees on a park bench and watched Mr. Moon light up the blue water of Matanzas Bay.

Life in the "Love" stage is idyllic.

14.

I was operating the cash register at the front counter when I heard a loud thump behind me. I turned around and saw Mr. M had collapsed and was lying on the floor. I and a customer ran over to him and we saw he was clammy and sweaty and had difficulty in breathing. His hands were placed over his heart. I told the customer to call 911, and I placed a jacket over him to keep him warm until the ambulance arrived. I knew from my Mom's heart attack that he needed CPR and aspirin. I didn't know how to administer CPR so I ran for the aspirin stored in the counter drawer and forced 2 pills in his mouth.

About 15 minutes later, two emergency medics arrived, looked at Mr. M, and one immediately initiated CPR and the other started a chest compression procedure trying to provide oxygen to his lungs. Mr. M. had stopped breathing. They hooked him up to a portable oxygen tank and stretchered him to the ambulance. I quickly locked the door of the shop and accompanied them in the ride to St Augustine Hospital.

When we arrived in the emergency room, a medical team immediately performed a PCI intervention procedure to get his heart breathing but to no avail. The emergency doctor informed me Mr. M suffered a massive heart attack and was dead on arrival. I don't recall anything else except getting dizzy and passing out. I later learned Frank and Mary drove me home.

15.

There was loud knocking on the door, and I opened it and see Victor.

"I heard about Mr. M, Ollie, so sorry. What a decent man he was."

"Yea, Victor, thanks, it happened so suddenly, just like my Mom. I must be star-crossed."

"Nonsense, Ollie, pure nonsense, you're just distraught now. Everything will be okay."

"Victor, I'm not sure what I am going to do now with the shop closed."

"Don't worry about that now, after the funeral we'll take a look at the bulletin board and find another job. Come on, let's go get you something to eat, you must be starved."

16.

The funeral mass at the Cathedral Basilica was packed with Mr. M's Knights of Columbus friends, and with many families of parishioners who knew Mr. M or the late Mrs. M. Monsignor Gatto conducted the service. After the readings from the bible were completed, the good Father offered a lovely personal eulogy of Mr. M. He and Mr. M had become close friends after the death of Mrs. M. He then announced that I had requested to say a few words.

I introduced myself and then spoke of my being hired to work in the "Mom and Pop Pizza Shop" and how over the years working together I grew to respect Mr. M. and to view him as the father I never knew. I described a number of different activities we did together on Sunday, our only closed-shop day. I then said that Mr. M filled my heart with peace and joy and that I would treasure every memory we shared. I closed crying: "Mr. Martini, I love you and will miss you, and I never will forget your kindness to me" and left the altar sobbing.

The mass was followed by interment near Mrs. M's grave at the local San Lorenzo Cemetery. At the site were Rosie and me, the Fernandez family, Victor and Margrete, and a stranger. The ceremonial rite at the cemetery was brief and ended with Msgr. Gatto's recital of a final prayer.

As we began to depart, the stranger approached me and handed me her card: Grace Doherty, Attorney-at-Law. She told me she was Mr. M's business attorney and I should call her when I felt ready, that she needed to discuss his Will with me. She apologized for meeting this way and explained her office was unsuccessful in locating me. She said my name and address was neither in St Augustine's phonebook nor in any other public record. I thanked her and said I would call her.

The terms of the Will were straight-forward. I was the sole heir, except for one bequest of $10,000 to Msgr. Gatto. I was now the owner of the house, the business, and all other assets, including his 2005 Hyundai Sonata. Ms. Doherty and I briefly discussed a number of options regarding the business and I told her I wanted to operate it. Before I left, she handed me an envelope with my name on it. In it was Mr. M's father's secret pizza sauce recipe that he brought with him when he emigrated from Italy in 1928.

17.

I left Ms. Doherty's office in a daze. Couldn't believe Mr. M. made me the sole heir of everything he owned, including his business. My dream goal in life was to be a successful entrepreneur and thanks to Mr. M, I was getting an opportunity to achieve it at the very young age of 20. I was determined to make him proud.

When I returned home, I immediately started focusing on the needs of the business. I thought of Mary first. She was an experienced short order chef at Flagler so I needed to talk to her about joining me at the shop. That was the most pressing need to continue the pizza business. Without a chef, I would have to close the shop or sell it, neither of which I wanted to do.

I telephoned Rosie and told her my plan. She called me back and said she and her parents were coming over to discuss it. I offered Mary the same generous offer Mr. M. extended to me: a 10% ownership interest in the business and a 20% increase in salary over her current one. Her quick response was "I can start after my two weeks-notice to Flagler is fulfilled." The four of us erupted with a cheer and I shook hands with Mary and Frank as symbolic acts of closure.

Next on my "To Do List" was to talk with Victor. He was graduating from the University of Florida and I called him to see if he wanted to join me in the business. He thanked me for the offer and reminded me that his goal was to become a doctor. He said he was accepted into the med school and was excited about it.

I then hesitatingly asked him if his Dad was attending his graduation. I knew I probably shouldn't have asked but as his best friend in the Town I was dying to know.

"I couldn't reach him on the phone, left messages inviting him, but received no call back." I told Victor I was sorry to hear that. He said he wasn't at all surprised and that he decided he would not attempt to contact him again. "Ollie, I'm just tired of beating myself up because of his lack of acceptance of me. So, here's some good news. Margrete and I are getting married before I start med school. It will be a 'quicky' by a local Justice of the Peace in

Gainesville." I congratulated him and agreed to stay in touch.

I closed the shop for two weeks. Rosie and I looked at each other and we both had the identical thought. Since it would be 2 weeks before we could reopen the shop and we were almost 21, why not get married during that period. So, we did. Msgr. Gatto performed the ceremony with only Frank and Mary, daughter Elena, and son Ernie as attendees. We then took off for the Gulf coast barrier island of Longboat Key where we honeymooned for a week, basking in the sun on its white sandy beach during the day and snuggling at night in our lovely suite at the Ritz.

18.

The "Mom and Pop Pizza Shop" reopened with me as cashier and with Mary as chef. Sales were a little sporadic at first but started to pick up in a couple of weeks once the public learned we had reopened. I had graduated from Flagler's business school and loved applying the abstract concepts and principles to the business. And, free from classes at night, I now channeled all of my time and energy into the business. Each day at the close of business, I started experimenting to create a new pizza product until finally deciding to test market a new product called the "Pizzawich." It consisted of two small 4" by 4" pizzas, with one of them inverted over the other forming a pizza sandwich. I reformulated "Grandad" Martini's sauce to a consistency similar to peanut butter so that the toppings adhered better to the pizza dough. The customer still could choose thin or thick pizza dough and the usual mozzarella, pepperoni, sausage, or veggie toppings. The sandwich would be packaged in an eco-friendly take-out container and I marketed the new product with the slogan:

"Gotta Pizza Itch, Try a Pizzawich"

And try they did. The new Pizzawich was a smashing success. Local social media was lighting up with favorable customer feedback. The "Mom and Pop Pizza Shop" was soon operating at full capacity 6 days a week with, at times, customer lines spilling out the door to the sidewalk. To handle the increased volume of phone orders, two 17-year-old boys from the Town were hired to join the team.

After many quarters of steady sales increases, I next decided that in order to take the business to a level beyond regional, I needed to attract a Shark on ABC's popular business reality TV show, "Shark Tank." [The Tank's panel of Sharks (investors) first listen to pitches from entrepreneurs seeking funds to expand their businesses and then each decides whether or not to make the capital investment.] I filed an application, passed the interview, and was invited to present. So I did, and the panel liked the new sandwich concept and were impressed with its sales volume and high profit margin. They even agreed the offering price of $300,000 for a 10% ownership in the business was fairly valued.

I gave each Shark a Pizzawich to sample and they were unanimous in liking the taste and ease of eating pizza as a sandwich. I was waiting optimistically for an offer. Suddenly, each of two Sharks back-to-back explained he was not interested in investing his money in the retail marketing of food items. Another Shark said she already had pizza in her investment portfolio so she opted out. One other opined that she was sorry but the brand was not broadly established enough for her to risk her capital in the business. However, much to my relief and to the surprise of the other Sharks, the final Shark said he loved it and offered the $300,000 for the 10% equity ownership interest in the business. I was ecstatic and quickly accepted his offer, sealed the deal with the customary Tank hug, and left after thanking the panel for the opportunity to present.

19.

After appearing on the Tank, our sales quickly shot upwards like a rocket blast at Canaveral. We had to either enlarge our physical space or open another shop. Mary and I agreed we needed to arrange a Zoom meeting with the Shark to discuss this new issue.

When the Zoom conference ended, I remarked to Mary "wow, that was impressive." She laughed and said "Ollie, he's a successful billionaire businessman so why wouldn't he know how to advise us."

"Yep, you're right, Mary, good point."

Here is what the Shark advised: "Move out of the house, convert the house solely to the business. Do it right by hiring an architect and a general contractor. Tell the architect to provide maximum eat-in space. (We will no longer be just a carry-out pizza place.) Also, design a new facade with the lower case slogan 'Home of the Pizzawich' under the upper case sign "MOM AND POP PIZZA SHOP." Purchase the lot across the street and ready it into a customer parking lot. Defray the expenditures with the $300,000 capital I bought in with and take out a mortgage for the balance. In addition to increased revenue, taking these steps will give us significant business tax write-offs."

While the renovation project was going on, I called Victor to see how med school was going and he said he was extremely busy but loved it. He then told me he and Margrete decided to return to St Augustine after med school to complete his residency here at the local hospital. "And now for the real news, Ollie, we have been blessed with a baby girl we named "Rosie." When I heard that I could barely utter another word I was so choked up. I ended the call by congratulating him and telling him I loved him like a brother and to stay in touch.

Checking my "To Do List" names, I then called Ernie who had recently graduated from Duquesne University's School of Business and was working for Alcoa in Pittsburgh. I told him of my need for help and offered a 20% raise over his current salary and an option sweetener to purchase 10% of the company stock, exercisable after one year. Being a bachelor, it was an easy decision for Ernie and he readily accepted my offer. He and I would be the cashiers.

I still needed another chef. Mary recommended a young single Black woman she worked with at Flagler, "who was experienced and dependable." So, I met with Ms. Joanne Harrington, liked her experience and personality, and offered her a position as the 2nd Chef, with the customary 20% raise over her current salary.

She was delighted with the offer and added, "I enjoy working with Mary so the job sounds perfect, thank you so much."

Great, the new team was now in place. The newly renovated "Mom and Pop Pizza Shop" was ready to roll. And it did. The Pizzawich was a sales sensation accounting for over 75% of the gross sales of the business and our total sales chart reflected a steady year-after-year upward trend line.

20.

Rosie, of course, loved the Shark's advice and quickly started looking for a new home. She found a house she liked on Dolphin Drive and I agreed it was perfect. It was a 3-bedroom stone ranch-style home with a 2-car garage, a cedar shake roof, and a back patio with a clear view of the traffic on the Intercoastal Waterway. The house was ideally located being only a short walking distance to, and over, the Bridge of Lions to the scenic Historic District and to the shop. Elena, Rosie's younger sister, also lived on Dolphin Drive, which added appeal to the location.

Rosie and I moved into our new home and enjoyed the extra square footage compared to the bungalow. The only damper was that Rosie and I were biologically unable to have children. Over the years, we were each tested and retested, clinic after clinic, one specialist after another, but to no avail. We had suffered in silence long enough and decided to adopt a boy from the Town. I contacted Father Augustine, who arranged interviews with 5 boys, ranging in ages from 10 to 14. We adopted a 12-year-old named Ronald. Rosie had been praying novenas for years asking for a child and her prayers were finally answered.

Our home exploded with joy with the arrival of Ronald. Boys Town had done its job well. He was like a miniature adult--- mature, neat, kind, and loving---in short, he was the proverbial icing on our cake of married life. Rosie and I just could not get enough of him. And I vowed to be the father to him that I never had.

21.

At the next annual shareholder meeting, we unanimously agreed with the Shark's recommendation that it was time to begin franchising our business model. We established the selling price and discussed the IP (Intellectual Property) and the other assets and services to be included in the "Mom and Pop Pizza Shop" franchise package. I volunteered to take the matter up with attorney Doherty and to engage her firm to handle the project.

The next decades passed seamlessly and productively. The "Mom and Pop Pizza Shop" template was successfully franchised throughout the States with the Pizzawich tradename obtaining national brand recognition. Net revenues rose exponentially and I had achieved my dream goal of becoming a successful entrepreneur. Rosie and I were now multi-millionaires, exceeding our wildest dreams.

Victor kiddingly started to call me Tom. When I initially asked why, he offered "Keep it up, and you may become another Tom Monaghan, the founder of "Domino's Pizza" who, like you, also lived in an orphanage."

Rosie and I agreed it was time to give back, so we donated $5 million to the local Boys Town for the furnishings and construction of a new stand-alone church on its grounds. We conditioned our gift on the placement of a permanent plaque on the front entrance of the church celebrating Father Augustine's lifetime contribution to Boys Town.

We are sitting on our patio after Sunday dinner enjoying a lovely May evening with a glass of chilled sauvignon blanc. Our life is in perfect harmony and balance, and I, swept up in the emotion of the moment, look at Rosie and whisper: "Ah, Rosie, if only my Mom and Mr. M could see us now."

"I am sure they can Ollie, and I am also sure they are proud of you."

"And, so am I," as she reaches outward and clinks her wine glass with mine.

THE END

EPILOGUE

Rosie and I established a charitable trust to donate funds annually to various charities. This year the trustee answered the call of a "Cry of the Orphans" campaign by gifting $3 million to a charity, whose sole purpose is to help orphans world-wide. I still manage the original shop near Flagler College and Rosie devotes her time and services to local charities and schools.

Our son Ronald is a graduate of Georgetown University. He married Victor and Margrete's daughter, Rosie, and is blessed with 2 daughters. He owns and operates a profitable "Mom and Pop Pizza Shop" franchise on M Street, NW, in Washington, D.C. His business team consists of mostly graduates of Boys Town.

He told me a couple of his Hoya buddies poked fun at his career choice...pizza? "Ron, you went to Georgetown to sell pizzas?"

"Yep, sure did. Good enough for my 'Pizzapreneur' Dad, It's good enough for me."

Our closest and dearest life-long friends, Victor and Margrete, live in the fashionable Historic District and we visit each other weekly and talk on the phone daily. Dr. Victor takes care of my extended family's medical needs and I take care of his extended family's pizza needs.

Frank Fernandez retired from the City Park Service so he was no longer obligated to live there to retain his job. He and Mary purchased a "forever" home on the barrier island of Anastasia with an Atlantic Ocean view and invited Rosie and me over to see it. Frank was beaming with pride. And the pride shifted to me when he said "Ollie, you work hard, obey the laws, pay your taxes, and this wonderful country called America rewards you with a quality life."

Their daughter Elena married a local tax attorney and has two children. Their son Ernie fell in love with 2nd Chef Joanne and married her after a very brief engagement period. Unlike Rosie and me, there was no intermediate "Loke" stage experience in their relationship. It went directly from "Like" to "Love."

AUTHOR'S NOTE

This is the second of my Orphan Ollie books.

ORPHAN OLLIE OPTS OUT

In the first book, Ollie, a sixteen-year-old orphan, opts out of his State's program of homes for orphans, and "escapes" to St. Augustine, Florida to attempt to make it on his own.

ORPHAN OLLIE OPTS IN

In stark contrast, this second Orphan Ollie book depicts Ollie heeding the advice of his parish priest and choosing the structured-mentoring home of Boys Town in St. Augustine, Florida.